Christmas Eve Blizzard

By Andrea Vlahakis
Illustrated by Emanuel Schongut

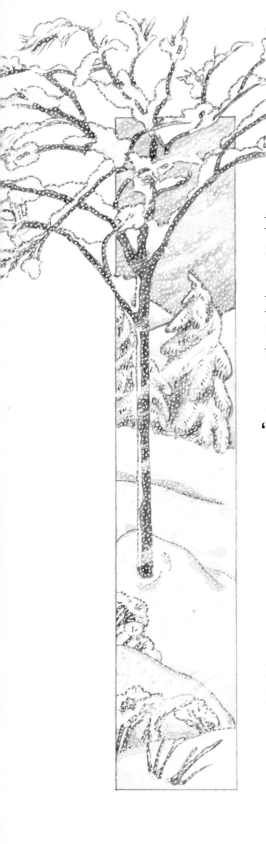

Snow fell all through the night and into the morning. Yet, Nicholas could still see the young apple tree from his window.

"It's only been seven months since we planted our apple tree, *Abuelo* (grandpa)," said Nicholas. "How will it make it through the storm?"

"That tree will still be standing long after this blizzard," said Grandpa Santos. "It was planted well."

"But it's so small," said Nicholas.

"*Sí*," Grandpa Santos agreed. "It's small but strong — with good roots to steady it. It will be fine."

Grandpa Santos headed for the hall staircase. "Tonight's Christmas Eve," he called out, "and the tree to concentrate on right now is the one down in the living room." His voice trailed, "We need to finish decorating it, Nicky."

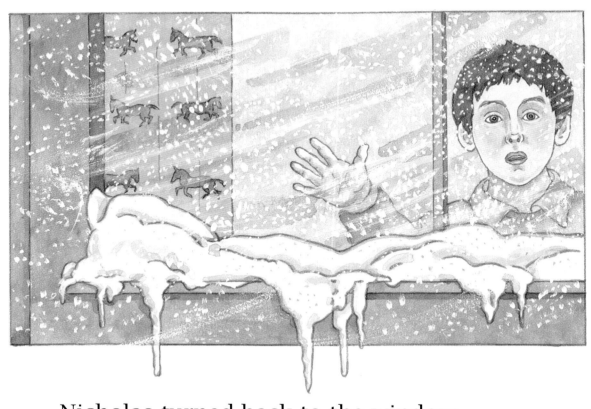

Nicholas turned back to the window.
Watching the snow fly furiously, he
saw a flutter of feathers. A bird
tumbled off an apple branch
onto a high drift of snow.
    "No . . ." Nicholas whispered.

He rushed into his boots and coat. He threw on *two* scarves, his hat and mittens and ran out into the storm.

From where he stood, Nicholas could easily
see the bird – bright red – by the apple tree.
Getting to the tree was something else.

Nicholas only took three steps before the wind blew him backwards into the snow. He struggled to his feet and pushed forward – first one step, then another – as he bullied back the wind.

When Nicholas looked up, snow pelted his face like little pinballs.

 In the distance, he noticed the bird wasn't moving. Nicholas put his head down and did not stop until he reached the apple tree.

 Snow had covered the bird's red feathers so quickly that they looked pink.

 He scooped the bird up and wrapped him in the second scarf. Following his own footsteps back to the house, Nicholas brought the bird inside.

"I should be very angry with you," said Grandpa Santos, "*muy enojado,* for going out in this blizzard." He looked at the bundled up scarf Nicholas was holding. "But . . ."

"*Abuelo*," said Nicholas, out of breath, "it's a bird." The scarf moved a little.

"He's still alive," said Nicholas.

"That, he is," said Grandpa Santos. "*Pobrecito* – poor little bird. Between not being able to find food in the storm and such cold weather, the blizzard almost did him in."

Nicholas loosened the scarf and held the bird up for his grandpa to see. "Isn't he beautiful?"

His grandfathers's eyes widened as he stared at the bird. "I haven't seen one since I was a little boy in Mexico..." Then Grandpa Santos said softly, "*Es cardenal.*"

"I've never seen a cardinal before."

"They don't usually live in this part of the country," said Grandpa Santos.

"But here he is," said Nicholas.

His grandfather nodded slowly. "To wander so far from their territory . . ." said Grandpa Santos, as if he was talking to himself.

"We have to help him," said Nicholas.

"That we do, Nicky." Grandpa Santos started to rig up a makeshift birdcage. "My grandfather used to say, 'When you do a good thing, good will come back to you.' "

Nicholas put a small bowl of water and a
sprinkling of birdseed in the cage.
    "You mean, like plant a tree?"
    "*Sí*, or rescue a cardinal." said Grandpa Santos.

The next day – Christmas morning – the cardinal was hopping around his cage, trying to fly out.

"He's regained his strength," said Grandpa Santos. "We have to let him go."

Nicholas nodded. "Will he stay here in Sawtooth Ridge?"

"*No sé*," answered Grandpa Santos. "I just don't know."

Before he unwrapped his presents, Nicholas took the birdcage outside and opened it up. The cardinal flew straight to the apple tree. He watched Nicholas for a few minutes, then flew off.

"Merry Christmas," Nicholas whispered.

All winter, Nicholas watched his apple tree. No cardinal came.

"He must have found his way back home," said Nicholas. "But we were lucky, *Abuelo*, weren't we? We got to see a cardinal."

"Oh, yes, Nicky, that we were," said Grandpa Santos.

Many years have come and gone now. Nicholas is a grown man. Grandpa Santos died twelve years ago. And as often as snowstorms happen in Sawtooth Ridge, there has never been another blizzard on Christmas Eve.

Although something else does happen . . .

People come from far and near to see the apple tree Nicholas and his grandfather planted all those years ago. But not because it is so old.

Because of something else.

From a distance, the tree looks like it is full with apples.

It isn't, though.

No one knows why it happens. And no one knows when it started.

Except Nicholas.

Because every Christmas Eve, his apple tree. . .

*fills with
beautiful
cardinals!*

For Creative Minds

Spanish/English Glossary

abuelo

grandfather

si - yes
muy enojado - very angry
pobrecito - poor little bird
no sé - I don't know

es cardenal

it is a cardinal

Cardinal (and Bird) Fun Facts

Birds are the only animals that have feathers. They have one bill, two legs, and a four-chambered heart. Like us (mammals), they are warm-blooded and breathe air. Birds lay eggs.

A male Northern Cardinal is usually recognized by bright red coloring. The female Northern Cardinal is grayish tan with red in the wings, tail and its crest. Both male and female adults have a red bill.

When the babies are 9 or 10 days old, they leave the nest. The male watches them and cares for them for about three weeks while the female sits on the nest with more eggs.

Many birds have different colorings depending on whether the bird is a male or female. Generally, males have brighter colors or markings to attract the females. The females tend to have duller coloring to help them hide (camouflage) as they sit on the nest.

The female sits on the nest, and the male brings food for her and the babies.

Cardinals migrate short distances.

Both cardinals raise their babies together. They usually have three or four babies at once and may have up to two or three sets (broods) of babies in the spring and summer.

Making a Bird-Happy Backyard Habitat

Just like us, birds need food, water, and a place to live. If they can find those things in your backyard, you might just have some birds move in as neighbors!

Birds need native food

Plant native trees, shrubs, grass, or flowers that will provide a variety of food like nuts, acorns, fruits, and nectar. Different birds like to eat and live in different types of plants.

Cardinals eat a variety of seeds. If you want to attract cardinals, plant things like:

Mulberries	Wild grape vines
Serviceberries	Virgina Creeper
Dogwoods	Black oil sunflowers (black seeds)
Crabapples	Safflowers

- If it will not damage the house, leave dead limbs on trees so birds can eat the bugs.
- Make a pile of dead branches that fall or yard clippings in an out-of-the-way area to attract birds.
- Use leaves and other autumn "fallings" as mulch in your winter gardens – it will attract birds and help your garden!

Birds need water to drink and to bathe

- Buy or make a shallow bird bath, (with no more than one inch of water) that rests on the ground. Place it near quick shelter, too, like a shrub or small tree in case cats are around.
- You could make a bath out of a heavy plastic lid or old garbage can lid. You can even use a terra cotta or plastic saucer from a plant pot!
- Birds really like dripping water which you can supply by hanging an old bucket with a small hole in the bottom over the birdbath. Make sure to change the water every few days to keep it fresh.

Birds need a place to sleep and build nests

- Some birds like to live high in the trees; others like to live low to the ground.
- Cardinals like to nest in dense hedges or thickets. They especially like nesting in honeysuckle thickets. They like living in various types of pine trees (evergreens) during the winter when it gets cold. If you plant trees, flowers or bushes to attract birds to your backyard, use plants that are native to your area.

Bird Feeders Are Not Just for Winter! Easy Crafts

There are several bird feeders that can be purchased and used. Different types of birds will eat out of different feeders. Cardinals like eating from platform feeders, but will also eat out of hopper feeders (with a tray) or tube feeders with big enough perches. Backyard birds like eating out of feeders all year long - not just during the winter.

1. Tree Garland

Using a heavy string, natural yarn, or twine and a blunt yarn-type needle, string the following bird treats. When finished, drape the garland in a tree or on a bush for the birds to enjoy.

Popcorn
Peanuts (in the shell) or other nuts
Crab apples

Slices of oranges or fresh berries
Dried fruit (any type)
Cranberries or raisins

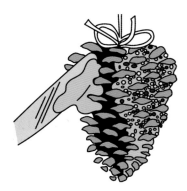

2. Peanut Butter Pinecones

Attach a heavy string, natural yarn or twine to the top of a pinecone. Cover the cone with peanut butter or suet (purchase at bird-feed stores), press sunflower seeds or a birdseed mix into the peanut butter or suet. Hang from a tree branch.

3. Bird Platter

Take an aluminum pie pan and punch several nail-sized holes in the bottom (for drainage). Place the tin on top of an old hanging plant container and hang from a tree limb or a pole or simply place the pan on top of a fence or deck post. Cardinals like eating about 5 to 6 feet off the ground. With enough drainage holes, the seeds should be okay through most rains. Change the seeds if they get too soggy and wet. An old plastic sand shifter toy could also be used.

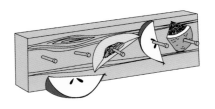

4. Bird Buffet

Hammer non-rusting galvanized nails into a piece of wood – leaving an inch or two poking out. Nail it to the side of a fence or a pole. Place pieces of orange, lemon, apple, pear, or peach on the nails.

What To Do If You Find An Injured or Orphaned Bird

If a bird is obviously injured or has something that looks like grains of rice in its feathers, take it to a wildlife rehabilitator right away. Poke several holes in a small box for ventilation, and line it with paper towels. Place the bird in the box, and carry it gently.

If a baby bird seems to have fallen out of the nest but is hopping around, it is probably just learning to fly. Put the bird in its nest if you know where it is and can reach it. Otherwise, put it in a bush (not a tree). If there are no bushes close by, you can use a small, shallow basket with some pine needles in the bottom. Tack it to the side of the tree and then put the baby in it. In all cases, keep cats and dogs inside and away from the bird. Watch it for two hours or until dark. If the parents have not returned for it in that time, take it to a wildlife rehabilitator.

Cardinal Numbers and Math Games

A "cardinal" number really doesn't have anything to do with birds – but it does use the same word! A cardinal number is a counting number. "Three baby birds learned to fly" has the cardinal number "three."

An "ordinal" number would be putting a number in a place or in order. "The third baby bird learned to fly" uses the ordinal number "third."

If one female and one male cardinal have three different broods (groups or sets) of babies and each brood consists of three babies, how many baby cardinals do they have?

For older children: If each of the original babies has the same number of babies, how many grand-babies birds would there be?

Thanks to Ann Shahid, Education Director, Audubon Center at Beidler Forest
(SC) for reviewing the For Creative Minds section for accuracy.

To my father, with whom I've planted many trees -- A.V.
For R.A.H. -- E.S.

Publisher's Cataloging-In-Publication Data
Vlahakis, Andrea.

Christmas Eve blizzard / by Andrea Vlahakis ; illustrated by Emanuel Schongut..

[32] p. : col. ill. ; 27 cm.

Summary: Join Nicholas and his grandfather as they push aside the thoughts
of decorating the Christmas tree to lovingly care for a cardinal trapped in the
snow of a blizzard on Christmas Eve. Christmas morning finds Nicholas more
concerned about the bird than opening his gifts.

ISBN: 9780976494331 (hardcover)
ISBN: 9781607181156 (pbk.)
Also as ebook featuring auto-flip, auto-read, 3D-page-curling, and selectable
English and Spanish text and audio
Interest level: 004-008
Grade level: P-3
Lexile Level: 610

1. Blizzards --Juvenile fiction. 2. Cardinals (Birds) --Juvenile fiction. 3. Blizzards
--Fiction. 4. Cardinals (Birds) --Fiction. 5. Birds --Fiction. 6. Christmas --Fiction.
I. Schongut, Emanuel. II. Title.

MLCM 2006/43953 (P)
[E]   2005921092

Manufactured in China, January, 2010
This product conforms to CPSIA 2008
Second Printing

Sylvan Dell Publishing
976 Houston Northcutt Blvd., Suite 3
Mt. Pleasant, SC 29464